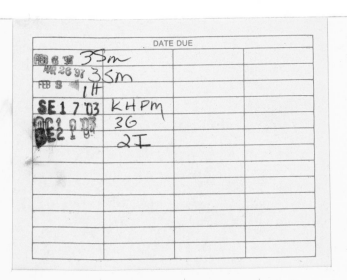

DATE DUE		
FEB 8 '91 3Sm		
MR 28 '91 3Sm		
FEB 3 1H		
SE 17 '03 KHPm		
OC 10 '03 3G		
OC 21 '03 2I		

E
STO

Stolz, Mary.

Emmett's pig

**ALLGROVE SCHOOL MEDIA CENTER
EAST GRANBY CT 06026**

Other I CAN READ Books®

EMMETT'S PIG

Pictures by Garth Williams

An I CAN READ Book®

EMMETT'S
PIG

by MARY STOLZ

HarperCollins*Publishers*

Library of Congress Catalog Card Number 58-7763
ISBN 0-06-025856-X (lib. bdg.)

for

Susan Penryth Carr

Emmett's
Pig

Chapter One

Emmett lived in the city.

He lived in an apartment.

The apartment was in a building.

And the building was near the park.

11

In the park there was a zoo.
Animals lived there.

There were lions, tigers, monkeys,
camels, seals, bears, and elephants.

12

There were also birds and fish.

And turtles.

But no pigs.

Emmett liked pigs.

He liked them better than birds and fish.

He liked them better than

lions, tigers, monkeys, camels,

seals, bears, or elephants.

Or turtles.

"Why are there no pigs in the zoo?"

said Emmett.

"They live on farms," said his mother.

Emmett said, "Farms are in the country."

"Yes," said his father.

"Where is the country?" asked Emmett.

"The country is outside of the city."

"Is it far?" asked Emmett.

"Pretty far," said his mother.

"Oh," said Emmett.

Then he said,

"Can we go to the country someday?

Can we go to the country

and see a pig?"

"Someday," said his father.

Some animals lived
in the apartment building.
Cats and dogs lived there.

Birds and fish lived there.

And turtles.

But no pigs.

"Mother, may I have a pig
in my room?" said Emmett.
"You have more than one pig
in your room," said his mother.
"You have all your toy pigs."

21

Emmett did have pigs in his room.

He had bank pigs, paper pigs,

wooden pigs, and glass pigs.

He had a pink stuffed pig

with yellow button eyes.

He had pictures of pigs.

He had books about pigs.

Sometimes he had pigs in his dreams.

But he had never seen

a real live pig.

"Mother," said Emmett,

"may I have a real pig in my room?"

"No," said his mother. "I am sorry."

"Why not?" asked Emmett.

"Because pigs live on farms

where there is a lot of space

and grass and dirt."

"I could have dirt in my room,"

said Emmett.

"My pig would think it was a farm."

"But you cannot

have dirt in your room,"

said his mother.

"Oh," said Emmett.

"Can we go and live on a farm?

So that I can own a pig?"

His father shook his head.

"My job is in the city, Emmett.

I am not a farmer."

Emmett went into his room to think.

He looked at all his pigs.

He liked them very much.

But he wanted a real live pig

more than ever.

He thought and thought

and thought about it.

He could not bring a pig to live

with him in the city.

He could not go to the country

where he could own a pig.

He did not know what to do.

Emmett said to his mother and father,

"I am going to be a farmer

when I grow up.

I am going to own a lot of pigs.

When the sun goes down,

I will sit on a stump

and admire all my pigs.

My special pig

will be named King Emmett.

King Emmett will not be

with the other pigs.

King Emmett will sit by me.

He will walk around the farm with me."

"That will be fine," said his mother.
"We will come
to visit you on week ends."

Emmett was pleased.

He went in his room

to look at his calendar.

He wanted to see how many days

were left in this year.

There were a great many.

And there were a great many years left

before he could be a farmer.

But Emmett did not think

about pigs all the time.

He had to think about school.

He had to think

about playing, and about books.

He had to think

about spaceships and firemen,

and about his friends.

He had to wonder

what makes an elevator go.

He had to wonder

how many glasses of water

to ask for when he went to bed.

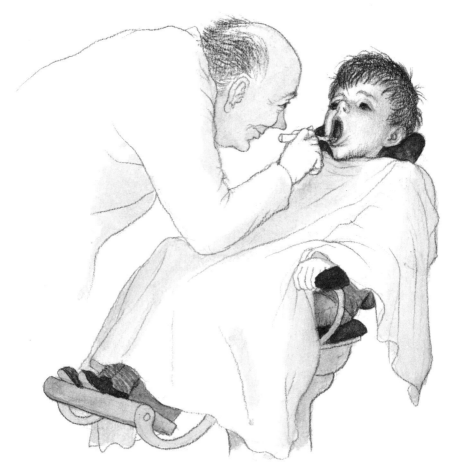

He had to go to school,

to the dentist,

to the house where his friend lived,

to the grocery store around the corner,

or just for a walk.

For a boy without a pig,

Emmett was very busy.

Chapter Two

One morning Emmett sat up in bed.

It was the thirty-first day of May.

It was Emmett's birthday.

Emmett got up and looked at his pigs

to see that they were all right.

They were all right.

He looked out of the window

to see if it was fine.

It was fine.

He went down the hall to see

if his mother and father were awake.

They were awake.

So his birthday began.

There were pancakes.

They were what Emmett liked

for a birthday breakfast.

There were present-shaped packages.

He ate the pancakes.

Then he opened the packages.

He got presents

from his two grandmothers.

He got presents

from his two grandfathers.

He got a truck and a ball and a puzzle.

He got a book to paint in.

He got a book to read.

He liked all his presents very much.

But he did not see any present

from his mother and father.

37

"Emmett," said his father

when the presents were all opened.

"We are going to take you

for a ride in the car."

"Yes," said his mother.

"We can call it a birthday ride.

There is a present for you at the end."

"From you?" said Emmett.

"Yes," said his mother and father.

"Can we go for the ride now?"

said Emmett.

"Right now," they said.

First they drove in the city.

"Is my present very far away?"
asked Emmett.

"Pretty far away," said his mother.

They drove through a tunnel.

"Is it in another city?" Emmett asked.

"No," said his father. "It is not."

40

They drove on a big highway.

"Is my present in the country?"

said Emmett.

"Yes," said his father and mother.

Emmett thought and thought.

"Is my present very small?" he asked.

"It is pretty small," said his father.

"Will it get bigger?"

"Yes," said his mother.

"It will get bigger."

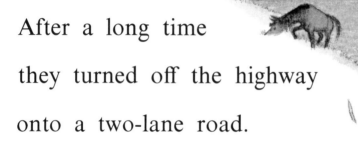

After a long time
they turned off the highway
onto a two-lane road.
Then they turned off the two-lane road
onto a dirt road.
They turned off the dirt road
onto a driveway.
They stopped in front of a farmhouse.
A man and a woman stood
waiting and waving.

"Hello, Mr. and Mrs. Carson.

This is our son, Emmett," said his father.

"How do you do?"

said Mr. and Mrs. Carson to Emmett.

"How do you do?" said Emmett.

He looked around the farm.

He saw a garden and a stable and a silo.

He looked past the silo,

and there was a beautiful pigpen.

It was white and clean.

"Shall we walk over there?"

said Mr. Carson.

"Oh, yes," said Emmett, and he ran.

In one part of the pigpen

there was a big mother pig

and some little pigs.

One of the little pigs

looked at Emmett.

One pig had nice little hoofs,

little pointed ears,

and round happy eyes.

He was round and shiny.

He stood on his little hoofs,

his small tail curled in the air.

And he looked right up at Emmett.

Emmett stood very still for a long time.

"It is a real live pig," he said.

"A real live pig," said his father.

"Is he really mine?" said Emmett.

"He is really yours," said his mother.

"He is your birthday present.

He will live here on the farm

but he will always be your pig."

"Well," Emmett said.

"Thank you. He is just what I wanted."

"We know," said his mother and father.

"My pig is named King Emmett."

"Oh," said his father.

"You are naming your pig after yourself?"

"Yes," said Emmett.

"Only he will be King Emmett,

so as not to mix us up."

"I see," said his father.

"It is the first time

we have ever had a king

living on our farm," said Mr. Carson.

"It is the first time we ever had a pig

boarding with us," said Mrs. Carson.

Emmett smiled. He said,

"I will send him a nickel

from my allowance. For a treat."

"Fine," said Mr. Carson.

"I am sure he will enjoy that.

And I will send you

a report card about him."

"He will be good," said Emmett.

"Shall I take him out?"

said Mr. Carson.

"So you can play with him?"

"Oh, yes, please," said Emmett.

So Mr. Carson lifted King Emmett

out of the pen.

King Emmett squealed.

He jumped to the grass and ran.

Emmett ran with him.

They ran all over the grass.

They ran past the silo and the stable.

They ran past the garden and the house.

Then they ran back again.

When they stopped running,

King Emmett came over

and sat down beside Emmett.

All afternoon Emmett

and his pig played together.

Now the sun was going down.

Mr. Carson put King Emmett back

with the other little pigs.

All the pigs began to eat.

Emmett sat on a stump to admire them.

Most of all he admired King Emmett.

King Emmett was the handsomest,

biggest, pinkest pig of them all.

King Emmett looked at Emmett.

"He knows you," said Mr. Carson.

"Yes," said Emmett. "He does."

Then Emmett and his mother
and father said good-by to the Carsons
and got in their car.
They drove back to the city.
It was late when they got home.
Emmett went right to bed.
He only asked for one glass of water.
Then he went to sleep very fast,
so he could dream about King Emmett.

The next day Emmett told the teacher
and all the children in school
that he owned a pig.

He also told the elevator man,

the grocery man,

the dentist,

and a man he did not know.

59

They all thought it was fine.

Even the man he did not know

said it was a fine thing

to own a real live pig of your own.

Emmett was very proud.

He was also very busy.

Every week he got

a letter from Mr. Carson.

Every week he wrote back,

and sent a message to King Emmett.

Once in a while he sent

a nickel of his allowance,

so that King Emmett

could have a treat.

He had a lot of other things

to think about,

and to do.

But mostly he thought

about the day when

he and his mother and father

would all drive back

to the country to visit his pig.

61

And every night he had a dream.

In this dream there was

a pig and a boy.

They were both named Emmett,

and they were very good friends.

THE END